PROBABILITY CHAIN

by R P Keeter

FIRST EDITION

Printed in the United States of America

ISBN: 978-0615861784

To my beloved wife,

without whom this story would not

have been possible.

As far as the laws of mathematics refer to reality,
they are not certain,
and as far as they are certain,
they do not refer to reality.
— Albert Einstein

CHAPTER 1

When the shape of a young woman began to materialize in the middle of the intersection at Peachtree and Piedmont, six lanes of traffic going more than forty miles-per-hour came to a screeching halt. Car slammed into car as space itself seemed to ripple, to stretch. Although translucent and fuzzy at first, she gained form quickly. And as she did, it became clear to all who could see her that she was badly injured, possibly near death. Hunched over and naked, she held her hands to her bloody neck while cars swerved, horns blared, and steel grinded against steel.

When later questioned by the police, only one of the drivers dared admit that the woman had appeared out of nowhere. The rest claimed they just hadn't seen her.

The answers, though disappointing, were no surprise to the officers. With streetlamps, headlights, lighted billboards, and neon signs making the darkness of night darker and the brightness of light brighter, drivers were often unaware of how little they actually saw once the sun went down.

But, while the question of her origin was important, it was not the question on anybody's mind in the moments that followed her appearance. Instead, the only question witnesses asked themselves as they stepped from their cars, slack-jawed, was whether this mysterious woman was going to live.

A mother dressed in khaki pants and a blue blouse grabbed a blanket from her trunk and ran toward the stranger, shouting, "Call an ambulance! Somebody call an ambulance, goddammit!"

She kneeled beside the young woman, wrapping the blanket around her and placing her hands on top of the stranger's throat to try to slow the bleeding.

As she did, the young woman looked up at her with desperate blue eyes. Her lips moved to form the name "Brian," but no sound came out.

CHAPTER 2

Several miles away, a heavy, deep thump from downstairs immediately woke Brian Dore. At first he tried to dismiss the sound as meaningless. John Flanders, both clumsy and old, was always dropping one thing or another.

But the sound, hazy and muted, like the dream-soaked, half-memory it was, left him uneasy. For the eleven years Brian had lived with John, he had worried that one day John's clumsiness would send the fragile seventy-five-year-old tumbling down the stairs, not to recover. And when another thump followed, he decided he should investigate.

A small reading lamp sat on the bedside table next to him. He turned it on.

He climbed out of bed and crept into the hall, dressed in his boxers and tee shirt.

He told himself that there was nothing to worry about. John had probably just slipped on the tile floor in the kitchen. Probably making a midnight sandwich when his thin legs came out from under him.

Yet that didn't feel right. Brian couldn't convince himself to call out for John, ask if he was okay. The uneasiness he'd felt upon waking had grown into a sinking, gnawing feeling twisting in his gut, warning him that the thump had been more than just a fall.

Trying to keep at bay the horrific thoughts that lurked just outside his consciousness, Brian eased quietly along the upstairs hallway. He couldn't bear the thought of something bad happening to the old man. Ever since Brian had moved in, John had treated him like a son, taken care of him, nursed him through the death of his parents.

Underneath the carpet, the floorboards squeaked only once. Brian froze, waited, then kept moving.

Next, he heard a clatter. *Could have been dishes.*

Then a crash. *That wasn't dishes.*

He picked up his pace.

Halfway down the stairs, he remembered the .38 Chief's Special underneath his bed. He cursed himself for not grabbing the gun when he had had the opportunity. But the truth was he rarely thought about it, had never used it. He didn't even know if it worked. He only had it because it had been his father's and was one of the few things left after the fire that had claimed his parents' lives.

Now, closer to the living room than his bedroom, he

dared not go back for it. If there were an intruder, moments were precious.

He started back down the stairs. Dark shadows obscured the den below. Only the faint trickle of light that bled through the window in the front door allowed him to see anything at all. He grabbed the handrail for support as if he might faint from fear.

Then he heard a rustling from the kitchen and more clanging: a waterfall of silverware crashing into silverware.

Once on ground level, he could tell that the den was thus far untouched by the intruder. Nothing was in disarray. Everything seemed to be accounted for, including the small TV John frequently watched.

Suddenly a flicker of light from the kitchen caught his attention. A flashlight.

His mind went into overdrive. He knew that whatever he was going to do, he was going to have to do it fast. Any hesitation could be dangerous, possibly deadly.

He swept into the den and grabbed the phone off a small table in the corner. Certain the line would be cut, he placed the receiver to his ear to check for a dial tone. He sighed with relief, punched 9-1-1, and dropped the phone onto the couch.

The operator would be able to trace the call. If nobody spoke, they would assume the worst.

Moving faster now, Brian grabbed Flanders' cane from the hall closet. The cane was made of solid oak and featured a brass handle.

Batter up, he told himself as he swung it over his shoulder, handle in the air. He crept down the hallway toward the kitchen. As he did so, he noticed the rustling sound move to the dining room and the light ahead fade.

Without the glow from the flashlight bouncing off the walls ahead, even the pictures on the faux wood paneling beside him were mere black on black shadows.

He inched forward through the darkness. As he closed the distance between himself and the intruder, his mouth went dry. His palms grew damp. Once he reached the kitchen, only a single doorway would stand between them.

Something on the floor . . .

At first, the thought barely registered. All he could focus on was the danger he was about to encounter.

Something big . . .

He took another cautious step forward, eyes still on the kitchen ahead. Then, the shadowy obstruction found its form and, for a brief moment, Brian stopped thinking about the intruder. For a brief moment, he stopped thinking about anything. He stopped breathing.

With fear gripping his throat, he barely acknowledged the clatter when the cane slipped from his hands and hit the ground. He pawed desperately for the light switch, flipped it.

As sixty blinding watts flooded the hallway, his fears were confirmed.

John Flanders was dead. In his bathrobe. His head was supported by one wall. His legs, bent up at the knee, were jammed into the other. Blood matted his hair, dripped down his face, pooled on the ground beside him.

Nearby lay a bloody wrought-iron candlestick. Brian recognized it as the same candlestick which, until tonight, had occupied a spot in the living room with other knick-knacks.

His hands shook. He stared at the body for a long time, unable to think. Everything around him faded away. In that moment, there was no past, no future, no kitchen before him, no living room behind him . . . just Flanders' body.

Then a sharp pain shot into his brain from the base of his skull and the world came back into focus. He reeled, caught himself before losing his balance, and turned around.

Holding the cane, the intruder took another swing at

Brian's head. This time he ducked. Instead of hitting its target, the brass handle tore a hole in the faux wood paneling.

The intruder was wearing khaki pants and a plaid shirt. He'd been smart enough to wear gloves, but hadn't thought to bring a mask. Not even a stocking to obscure his oversized nose and round cheeks. Nothing to hide his quivering brown eyes or greasy black hair.

Subconsciously, Brian understood that it was his lack of preparation that made him so dangerous now.

The burglar jerked the handle out of the wall to take another swing.

Brian jumped back as it took a chunk out of the opposite wall. He lost his balance and fell.

Clearly, the intruder intended on killing him, just as he had John.

Brian could only thank God that the psycho hadn't come with a gun or he would already be dead.

The gun . . .

His father's gun . . .

If he could get to it . . .

Before he could finish his thought, the intruder swung the cane again. Brian rolled onto his side, as close as he could to the wall, just before the makeshift weapon crashed to the floor.

He knew one more blow from the cane wouldn't kill him, yet it was proving to be as dangerous a weapon as he had expected.

Quickly, he rolled to his feet and backed up several steps, trying to get distance without turning around.

The intruder leapt over the body between them.

Heart pounding, mind blank—no longer thinking or worried about his dead friend, motivated only by his desire to survive—Brian turned to run. But not fast enough. The cane smacked him across the chin. Tearing flesh. Rattling his jaw. Sending him into a spin.

Again, he couldn't keep his feet under him. He fell onto his chest. The impact forced the breath out of his lungs.

A moment later, the cane struck his shoulder, inches from his head. Pain shot up his neck, down his arm. He was lucky the blow hadn't found his skull or he would certainly be unconscious.

But he knew where the next blow would land. He had one last chance for escape. While the intruder raised the cane high, gaining power for the next swing, Brian rolled onto his back and kicked one leg into the air. He caught the intruder in his chest, knocking him away. Then he scrambled to his feet and ran as fast as he could. Past the front door, up the stairs, into his room.

He grabbed a small wooden chair from the corner and wedged it under the door handle. Flanders had only furnished this room with a chair for aesthetic reasons. Except for the rare occasion Brian had used it as a clothes hanger, it had served no other purpose. Until now.

Now it was the only thing standing between him and a violent death.

With the few moments of safety the chair allowed, Brian turned on the overhead light, ran to the bed, collapsed to the floor, and pushed himself against the wall. His head and shoulder throbbed from the previous blows.

The 911 operator had certainly assumed the worst . . .

But what if she hadn't?

The door handle turned. The chair buckled slightly, but held its ground. Then there was a loud thud and the door vibrated violently.

Brian wasn't sure if the intruder had used the cane or his body weight to try to break through. But he knew the door was cheap, hollow. It wouldn't hold up long.

He reached under the bed for the gun. If he had to kill the man, he would. Even if he didn't have to, he might. He could live with the consequences.

John Flanders had been more than just his guardian. He had been Brian's closest friend and confidant. Killing the man who had taken his life would be nothing short of justice.

Another blow to the door.

His hand searched the area where the weapon should be. No gun. Instead, he felt a small piece of paper, probably a receipt that had fallen out of his pocket.

He bent down to look under the bed.

The gun wasn't there!

The receipt, which was sitting exactly where the gun should be, was actually a folded note with his name scribbled on it. The handwriting was very similar to his own, but he knew it wasn't his. Familiar somehow, though not his.

The door vibrated again from another hit.

He grabbed the note, unfolded it, and read the only line that it contained: *The police will get here in time.*

Under different circumstances, this mysterious note might have led him to thoughts about the role fate plays in our lives, about the relationship between destiny and coincidence. But with another thud on the door, wood splintered, revealing one shiny corner of the cane's handle, and his mind went into overdrive as he tried to figure out how he was going to escape.

CHAPTER 3

The police will get here in time.

Brian barely had time to ponder the implications of the note before another blow left a fist-sized opening in the hollow door.

He checked the phone by his bed to see if the 911 operator might still be there, but heard only the beep-beep-beep of a line that had been out of use too long.

Another crack of the cane. More wood splintered from the hollow door. Two more blows and the intruder got his arm through.

Brian scampered over to the windows, still clutching the note. Quickly, he freed the latch and tugged at the handles. Paint had sealed the frame. On the other side of the room, the intruder was pulling at the back of the chair in an attempt to dislodge it. Adrenaline coursed down Brian's arms as he tugged at the window again.

It raised an inch.

The legs of the chair thumped and rattled and then the chair slid to the floor. But before the burglar could open the door and kick it out of his way, Brian managed to get the window all the way open.

He crawled out onto a narrow overhang, glancing back only once.

For a brief second, the intruder had stopped, as if deciding whether to follow Brian into the night. His jaw was clenched.

This was supposed to be a routine burglary, Brian figured.

Just before the intruder decided to give chase, Brian wondered if he should have gone out the front door instead of upstairs. But with the pursuit again on, there was no time to speculate, no use in second-guessing himself. He scrambled down the overhang and readied himself for the twelve-foot jump onto the lawn.

Despite the cold air, tiny beads of sweat formed on his forehead. He looked back at the intruder, who was still inside the house. He tightened his hands into fists. *You can do it. Come on. You can do it*, he told himself. He'd never had any survival training and knew how to manage his landing only from what he'd seen on TV. One mistake and he might break his leg or his wrist. Or worse.

What other options did he have, though? There was no one out walking this time of night. No passing cars he could call to for help.

So he jumped.

Went limp.

His feet hit the ground first. None of his joints were locked. He folded in on himself. Rolled once.

Every bone and muscle hurt, but he didn't think anything was broken.

He got to his feet as quickly as he could and backed up until he could see his window. The intruder was only halfway out.

Finally, he heard sirens.

In his boxers and tee shirt, Brian ran to the street while the intruder retreated into the house. Waving his arms, realizing for the first time he had dropped the note somewhere, Brian flagged down the two black-and-whites. "A burglar," he said once the four officers were out of their cars, "killed John Flanders." This was the first time he had spoken since he'd seen the body. His voice trembled with every word.

"He's still inside?"

Brian nodded.

All four officers pulled their guns. They charged into the house shouting, "Police!"

#

The cops searched the house, repeatedly announcing their presence and encouraging the burglar to surrender. They made mental notes of the damaged door upstairs, the body in the hall, the open rear door, and the broken window inside it.

Outside, Brian waited. He slowly became aware of the chilly night air as goosebumps appeared on his arms and legs. Neighbors turned on lights, stepped out onto porches. Flanders' quiet street was alive with an excitement it had never known before.

Don't think about the body, Brian told himself, trying to shut out the memory of Flanders' bludgeoned skull.

Don't think about the body.

The blood matted in his hair.

Don't think about . . .

"Are you all right, kid?" asked a cop from behind.

A few moments earlier, the officer had come out of the front door and used the radio in his car to broadcast the homicide. Brian hadn't noticed. Startled, he whipped around. He took a deep breath and said, "Yeah, I'm fine. I guess."

"You look a little beat up."

The cop was talking about the wound on his face, Brian realized. Instinctively, he touched his chin. Blood came off on his first two fingers, but not enough to worry him. "It's just a cut."

"We can take you to a hospital."

"I'll be fine."

"Your choice. Anyway, listen, we're going to have to tape off the house. We'll have a forensics team down here soon, and I'm sure a homicide detective will want to talk to you."

Brian glanced around, dazed, swimming in the memory of Flanders' dead body again. "Where are the others?"

"Excuse me?"

"The other cops. There were four, now there's just you." He knew he sounded foolish for asking, but the strange note he had found left him questioning almost everything. He needed confirmation that there had, in fact, been four cops to answer the call. Because if there had only been two, one for each car, then maybe the murder wasn't real and maybe that strange note didn't exist and—

"They're around back. They're still searching for the suspect. Listen, I'm going to go get some clothes for you so you can get dressed, okay? After that . . . well, I'm going to need you to stick around for a while."

Brian nodded. "Sure. Yeah." Then he glanced back at all the neighbors watching the action. "I probably should put on some clothes."

"Where's your room?"

"Top of the stairs. First bedroom you come to."

The cop nodded. "I can pack a small bag for you if you want. You won't be able to get back into the house for a few days."

"Thanks."

"You got any neighbors who would let you stay with them, kid?"

He did, but he wasn't in the mood to discuss the tragedy with his neighbors. Anybody who took him in would keep him up all night with questions. "I'd rather stay in a hotel."

The cop grunted something unintelligible that might or might not have been sympathetic. Then he hoisted up his belt in an unconscious display of authority and disappeared into the house.

When he returned, the cop was carrying a duffle bag. He directed Brian to his vehicle and opened up the back door. "Climb on in, kid. You'll be more comfortable there than you would be standing around out here. Somebody will be by in a little bit to talk to you."

Brian did as he was told.

The cop handed Brian the duffle bag and walked away.

Mind blank, door open, clutching the duffle bag as if Satan might try to take it from him just as he had taken Flanders, Brian sat. Waited. Behind him, flashing blue and red lights bounced off the two-story Victorian home, a pair of uniforms ran yellow police tape around the property, an ambulance came and left, a forensics team went to work . . .

#

Brian wasn't sure how long he had been sitting in the back of that car before Detective Eric Donaven asked if he could have a word. All he knew for certain was that enough time had passed for most of his neighbors to lose interest and go back inside.

"Sure," Brian said, as emotionless as a machine. The numbness inside still had a chokehold on his pain. Dressed in a tee shirt and jeans, he got out of the car, reluctantly leaving his duffle behind, and shoved his hands into his pockets.

Detective Donaven was a tall man in his late thirties. He was thin, with shallow cheeks and blond hair. Dark, bloodshot eyes betrayed his otherwise spotless appearance — he hadn't sleep well in some time. However, his suit was pressed, his shirt freshly dry cleaned, and his tie was knotted in a double Windsor and pulled to the collar.

In contrast, his partner, Mark Divowlsky, was heavyset, with a round face and a double chin. His movements were slower than Donaven's, and stains on his shirt suggested that he didn't care for his clothing with the same fastidiousness.

"Tell us what happened," Donaven said.

"Well, I was upstairs sleeping when a . . . a thud . . . downstairs woke me up. When I went down to investigate . . . I saw this flashlight moving in the kitchen. That's when I knew . . . for sure . . . something was wrong."

Divowlsky lit a cigarette. "What'd you do then?"

"Well, I had to do something, because I was afraid that something might happen to John if I didn't."

"John?" Donaven asked. "He's . . ."

Brian nodded.

"John what?"

"Flanders."

Donaven scribbled something on a notepad. "He own

the house?"

"Yes."

"You two related?"

"Uh, no."

"How long have you lived here?"

"Since I was thirteen."

"Thirteen, huh? Where are your parents?"

"John is my guardian. My parents are dead."

"How'd that happen?"

"There was a fire," Brian said, trying not to visualize the ugly aftermath: the charred walls, the torched furniture . . . trying not to remember the nauseating smell of melted plastic that had soaked into the pores of the house.

For months after the accident, Brian had blamed himself for not being home when it happened, but the psychiatrist John had taken him to twice a week had explained there was nothing he could have done to help his parents. The fire appeared to have started in the kitchen. Probably someone had been cooking and had left the stove unattended. From there, the blaze spread up the wallpaper and quickly consumed the house. The autopsy report showed they'd both succumbed to smoke inhalation while trying to make their way down from the second floor. Inevitably, the flames reached them before the firemen could.

Had he been home, he'd likely be dead, too.

"I'm sorry for your loss," Donaven said, solemnly.

"So what did you do when you got downstairs?" Divowlsky pushed.

"I called nine-one-one and . . . and got his cane out of the closet."

"Thinking of taking a stroll?" Divowlsky chuckled at his own joke. His partner shot him a disapproving glance.

To Brian, Donaven said, "Don't pay any attention to him. Go on."

"Anyway, I started down the hall. From the sounds, I could tell the burglar had moved into the dining room. But it made more sense to me to go around, to come up behind him. So I did."

"Armed with a cane," Divowlsky said.

"It was the best weapon I could find."

"Maybe I'm dumb as cow's milk, but I don't get it. If you'd called nine-one-one, why not just duck out of the way and wait for the police to get here? Why go hunting some burglar, who may or may not be armed, with a walking stick?"

Angered by Divowlsky's rude comment, Brian looked up from the sidewalk to meet the detective's eyes.

"Because I wasn't sure they'd get here in time."

His gaze drifted away. After several quiet seconds, he continued. "The hallway was dark. I couldn't see the body until I was almost on top of it."

Donaven made another note.

"That's when the burglar attacked. He almost killed me right there in the hallway, but I ran. Upstairs into my room."

"Not outside?"

"Not yet."

"Why not?"

The gun.

"I don't know. . . . Anyway, I shoved a chair under the doorknob. But he just kept pounding at the door until he could get his arm though and push the chair away. So that's when I ran out the window onto the overhang and jumped onto the yard. Then your guys showed up. I think he would have followed me out to the street if the sirens hadn't scared him off."

The detectives glanced at each other. Divowlsky dropped the butt of his cigarette on the sidewalk, crushed it under his toe, and lit another. "You're a lucky boy."

Brian said nothing.

"So you've been here since you were thirteen,"

Donaven confirmed.

"Uh-huh."

"How old are you?"

"Eighteen."

"Been to college?"

"Not yet."

"Have a job?"

"An internship."

"Where's that?"

"Omega."

"Good company." Another note.

Had Brian been in a better mood, he would have agreed.

Omega Medical was one of the leading drug manufacturers on the East Coast. However to refer to Omega as just a drug manufacturer, as most people did, misrepresented the scope of the company's work. While it was true that Omega was best known for the development of specialized nerve medications, its staff had, since its inception seventeen years ago, also been involved in cancer research and partnered on explorations into alternative medicines.

Brian had been proud when he was offered an internship in the public relations department. So had John.

The opportunity to intern at Omega was rare, especially for someone who hadn't graduated college.

"So you were upstairs when you heard a thud," Divowlsky added, ready to get back to the matter at hand.

"That's what I said."

"And it woke you up. . . ."

#

The questions rolled in circles and doubled back on themselves until Brian began to cry. "Can we finish this later?" he asked, his voice cracking. He wiped away his tears and added, "I've already told you everything I know about this. Please, if you want to keep asking me the same questions over and over, can we finish it later? It's been a rough night. I mean, I'm not a suspect, am I?"

Before Divowlsky could tell Brian that this was their investigation and that they would ask as many questions as they felt like asking, Donaven closed his notepad and said, "I understand." He took a handkerchief from his coat pocket and handed it to Brian.

"Thanks."

"Wait a second," Divowlsky said. "We're not done here."

"For now we are."

"*I'm* not done here."

"Give it a rest, Mark. He's right. He's not a suspect. He's been more than cooperative and he's had a really rough night."

"This is ridiculous. Who's running the investigation here?"

"Mark, why don't you go see what sort of progress forensics has made?"

Divowlsky took a long drag off his cigarette and stormed off.

"Don't pay too much attention to him," Donaven told Brian once his partner was out of earshot. "He's a good investigator, but he's not very compassionate."

"Why's he such a jerk?"

"Just the way he was made," Donaven said. "Come on." Then he started walking toward an unmarked brown sedan.

"Where are we going?"

"You wanted to stay in a hotel tonight, right?"

"I've got a car."

"You're in no condition to drive." He opened up the passenger door. "Come on."

Brian took one last look at the house caged behind

yellow police tape. Blue and red lights reflected off its siding. Moving in and out of the front door, officers busied themselves with a variety of tasks.

At that moment, though he couldn't say why, Brian suddenly knew that things were going to get worse.

"Whenever you're ready," Donaven said.

With zero desire to linger, Brian was ready. He got his duffle bag out of the back of the police car and joined the detective in the sedan.

They pulled out onto the road. Donaven asked, "What hotel do you want to go to?"

"There's an Embassy Suites on Clifton."

"Yeah, I know it."

As they traversed the city, neither of them said a word. The only sound in the car came from the relentless static and fuzzy voices on the police radio. Outside his window, Brian watched the endless procession of street lamps until his tears dried up. When the silence became too much for him, he said, without turning his head, "John was a good man."

Donaven, unsure if Brian was talking to himself or to him, replied anyway. "I'm sure he was."

"He used to be a doctor."

"A noble profession."

“Everyone liked him. All the neighbors . . . everyone.”

They turned right onto Clifton.

“Sounds like a great man.”

Then the car fell silent again. The silence seemed to swell with pain, making the air thick, hard to breathe.

Donaven rolled down his window to let in a fresh breeze. The pressure in the car subsided some.

“Try to get some sleep,” the detective said after pulling up in front of the hotel and giving his passenger a business card.

Brian got out of the car, smiled weakly back, and said he would. He dropped the handkerchief on the passenger seat and, with his duffle bag slung over one shoulder, went into the lobby.

CHAPTER 4

It was going on two-thirty A.M. The tragedy had already sucked three hours out of Brian, but now—instead of sleeping—he was sitting in his hotel room, mindlessly watching TV. Some sort of low-budget thriller about the drug trade. A guy on the screen, whose name he hadn't caught, had just filled a cut-off latex finger with cocaine and swallowed it to get the drugs through customs.

During the commercial break, his eyes drifted to the bottle of pills on the dresser.

The concierge had given him a sealed, brown envelope when he checked in and he'd found the bottle of pills inside.

"Here. Somebody left this for you."

As he studied the bottle, wondering who had left it, his mind retreated from reality to an almost dream-like state, plunging him back through fractured memories until it latched onto a conversation at the office earlier that day. Talk of a new drug. Very hush-hush. Nobody knew exactly what it was, what it did, but there were theories. . . .

"I don't know what they call it," said Shawn Ryder, an employee in the PR department. Then, hovering around Brian's desk, he glanced over his shoulder to make sure nobody was listening. "But I've heard it does wild things."

"Like what?"

"Jerry, you know, one of the janitors, thinks it might be like LSD, only way more intense."

"What would Omega be doing making something like LSD?"

Shawn picked up the stapler off Brian's desk and played with it nervously. Most of the staff had already heard this story, but Brian knew that Shawn liked pretending they hadn't. "How should I know? Omega's into all kinds of stuff."

"Nothing against Jerry, but I don't think he's qualified to make these sorts of assumptions. Neither are we."

Shawn's face scrunched up tight with frustration. He put Brian's stapler down and leaned forward on the desk. Keeping his voice at a whisper, he said, "Well, whatever it is, it sounds damn interesting, I'll tell you that for sure."

Then Kerri White, the redheaded manager of the PR department, stopped by Brian's desk to deliver a press release. "It sounds like science fiction to me, boys. Omega wouldn't waste its time with something like that." She spoke with a smile that showed all her teeth and was wearing a skirt that showed most of her legs. Everyone knew she had gotten the job for her looks, but she'd since proven to be as smart as she was beautiful.

Shawn jerked his head around. He hadn't heard anyone coming and was surprised to see her there. "Well, of course you'd say that."

"Jerry's a halfwit who overheard some midnight conversation and took it out of context."

Shawn scoffed in her direction, but said nothing. He and Kerri had never gotten along. She was too levelheaded for him and never took part in his conspiracy theories.

"By the way, the drug's called Diaxium," she said, just before leaving. "That is, if you believe Jerry."

Although the container on the dresser probably didn't contain Diaxium, there was no name printed on it. It could have been anything.

There was also a note inside the envelope. Written on hotel stationary, the note said simply: *Take one as soon as you can. Trust me. A friend.*

The same handwriting from the note under his bed.

Even though the first one had accurately told him the police would arrive in time, he had not yet decided whether to trust this mysterious prophet.

He knew I would go for the gun. He knew I would come to this hotel. What does he want? How could he know?

But it was not just the unexplainable notes and the vanishing gun that alarmed Brian. It was also, to a lesser degree, his missing cash. While he had expected to pay for the room with a credit card, he hadn't expected to be missing the twenty dollars he'd gotten from an ATM earlier that day.

He glanced from the TV to the pills to the TV to the pills.

I don't know what they are.

He thought about Flanders' bloody skull and his parents dead on the stairs . . .

I don't even know where they're from.

. . . the flames burning up the wallpaper, consuming the ceiling . . .

They could be dangerous.

. . . the closed caskets at the funeral . . .

In the mood I'm in now, I . . .

. . . the charred remains of the house . . .

. . . shouldn't . . .

. . . and he wished he'd never stopped taking the anti-depressants the psychiatrist had prescribed for him after his parents died. When Brian's life had transitioned out of the darkness of loss, when he had started thinking not about a future of what might have been, but of what might be, the doctor had weaned him off the medication.

Now he needed them more than he ever had. And if he couldn't get them, he needed something, anything, to take away his pain. Cyclobenzaprine, dopamine, nortriptyline, doxepin, anything! Suddenly he wanted to trust this strange prophet.

. . . mustn't . . .

Could it really be that much worse than reality?

No, it couldn't.

He lunged for the container of pills and shook one out into his trembling hand. Discovering they were chalky to the touch, he chased it down with a glass of water from the bathroom sink.

He needed to escape, just for a little while. No matter where he went, no matter what sort of dreams he'd have, he needed to get away from his thoughts.

He put the "Do Not Disturb" sign on the exterior door handle to make sure nobody would walk in on him. Then he sat on the edge of his bed, waiting for the drug to kick in.

Five minutes passed.

He remembered the bloody candlestick.

Sweat broke out on his brow. He began to worry he had made a mistake by taking the pill.

Before he had a chance to dwell on it, though, his stomach clenched. He lurched forward, hands wrapped around his torso. Then he fell to the floor and started to spasm. His throat seized up. Suddenly, he couldn't breathe. The convulsions grew worse. His heart raced. His eyes rolled back. The room disappeared into blackness.

When the seizures stopped, unconsciousness followed.

CHAPTER 5

Brian was overcome with the need to vomit when he awoke. The uncontrollable urge welled up from his gut. He pushed himself onto his hands and knees. Stomach acid and chunks of food burned his throat as he expelled the filth onto a dirty cement floor.

Accompanying some sort of harsh, industrial music, he could see flashing strobes against his closed eyelids, and then, eyes open, the cracked cement underneath him.

Immediately, he realized he was no longer in his hotel room. Equally disturbing, he also realized he was naked.

As his gaze followed the cracks in the floor outward, he saw he was surrounded by an assortment of shoes he couldn't identify. Many were made of thick, black leather, reminiscent of Army boots.

He wiped his chin, lifted his head.

The men and women around him were dirty. Most wore clothes made of leather or cotton that had been cut close to the body and showed signs of age. Sleeves were unraveling. Pants were torn.

Nearby, water dripped through a hole in a pipe, forming a puddle.

Where was he? What had happened to him?

The drug.

None of this was real. It couldn't be. He was dreaming.

The breeze shifted. He smelled rotting meat. His stomach turned, but he didn't get sick.

Staring and pointing, the imaginary people chatted among themselves. But with the music overhead deafeningly loud, he could not hear what they were saying.

Then a young woman stepped forward. She kneeled beside him. She was dressed in tight leather pants that had a rip down one thigh, a leather jacket, and a gray shirt made of burlap . . . or something like it. She tucked her long black hair over her shoulder. *"Su bastu di?"* she shouted at him in a language he couldn't understand.

She waited while he rotated on his knees to face her. When he didn't answer, she grabbed his right hand and turned it over to look at the back of it.

The music stopped. No house lights came on.

"Lo nisti?" asked someone from the crowd.

"Nal lati lo," she answered.

"What are you saying?" Brian asked.

Before she could respond, if she even understood him, the east wall exploded inward. Cinderblocks crumbled as clouds of dust filled the air. Half-a-dozen motorcycles, mounted with blinding headlights, roared through the opening.

People around him screamed and scattered in all directions. They pushed past each other, around each other, and trampled the fallen in an attempt to escape. Shots were fired and somebody howled in pain as a bullet tore through his thigh.

The woman grabbed Brian's arm. *"Hord da li,"* she insisted. *"Hord da li!"*

From her tone, he translated that as "Come with me," and he did.

As she pulled him to his feet, he realized his legs were almost too weak to run. He struggled to keep up. Had she let go of his arm at any point, he would have lost her. He would have fallen behind, dropped to his knees, been trampled like so many others.

His heart pounded with fear. He tried to remind himself none of this was real. After it was all over, he would be back in the hotel room where he started, he told himself. Back with the loneliness and the pain . . .

When gunfire whizzed past nearby, his fear put a halt

to these thoughts.

The woman led him behind the bar and pushed aside a liquor cabinet to reveal a hole in the floor. She threw herself feet-first through it like she'd done it a thousand times and shouted at him—to follow, he assumed. He did, albeit much less gracefully.

They landed inside a tunnel. The woman grabbed a thin slab of cement off the ground. With one quick motion, she used the iron handle on the bottom to twist it into the hole like a screw. She pulled a small flashlight from her boot. As she did, he noticed something taped to the back of her hand. Then she grabbed Brian's arm again and continued to run.

The cement hallways were narrow, making him feel claustrophobic. But all too soon she led him up a ladder, through a small grate, onto the street outside.

The city looked like a war zone. Buildings were crumbling. The streets were dirty. Neon signs flashed from behind bared windows. Trash, caught in drafts, blew aimlessly. Many streetlamps didn't work; others just flickered. At night, the city was scary. If it had been real, Brian would have been absolutely terrified.

Panicking, he was unable to absorb any details before another explosion cracked the walls of the club behind them. They ran. Fast.

After several blocks, she pointed to a distant building and said something else in that strange tongue. However, as before, he was able to discern meaning from her tone and gestures. That building was their destination.

Unfortunately, the farther they went, the weaker he felt. His stomach started to turn again. The blood rushed out of his legs. He dropped to all fours only a block from the building. The shaking started. The spasms came soon after.

"Traca cano sta do? Traca stor?"

His eyes rolled back in his head and everything disappeared.

CHAPTER 6

Brian awoke to a loud *BANG! BANG! BANG!* on the door of his hotel room. It was relentless—and magnified by his throbbing headache. He rolled to his knees. Before he could speak, his stomach turned. Acid burned up into his throat as he hung his head over the side of the bed, but nothing else followed.

Like in his dream, he was naked. His clothes lay haphazardly on the floor nearby. The TV was still on, canned laughter pouring out of tiny speakers.

From the other side of the door: "Brian, this is Detective Donaven! Open up!"

Morning already? He staggered to the door through the sun-bleached room. Squinting eyes and voice hoarse, he said, "Let me put some clothes on, all right? Just a second."

The banging stopped.

Brian turned off the TV, grabbed his clothes, and sat down on the end of the bed. After dressing in everything but his socks, he noticed the dirt caked to the bottoms of his feet. Street dirt. It must have gotten there after he jumped out of his bedroom window.

How he wished he had time for a shower.

Donaven: "Come on, hurry up!"

He slipped on his socks and was about to get the door when he saw the bottle of pills. He didn't want to have to explain anything, so he hid them inside the top dresser drawer.

"Where the hell were you yesterday?" Donaven asked, after Brian finally let him in.

"What do you mean?"

"I mean Divowlsky and I came by, just like I told you we would. We knocked on this door until we just about broke it down. Finally, I had to get the front desk clerk to let us in. You weren't here."

"What day is it?"

Donaven put his hands on his hips, pushing back his suit jacket as he did so. Clearly he was not in a good mood. "Tuesday. What day do you think it is?"

The murder had happened on Sunday night. The only way it could be Tuesday is if he had been unconscious for more than thirty hours. "You must have had the wrong room."

"Don't play games with me. I'm not in the mood."

If you'd had the right room, you would have found me on the bed. Naked. . . . When did I take off my clothes?

"Well, I'm here now. Where's your partner?"

"He couldn't make it."

Brian nodded. "So you want to go through the questions again?" His eyes had adjusted to the sunlight, but he was still tired and his head still ached.

"Don't need to. Something's come up."

"What?"

"You know a girl named Raven?"

Brian thought hard, back through his memory. "No."

"Yeah, well, she knows you. She wants to talk to you real bad, too. She's down at Piedmont Hospital in ICU. Came in Sunday night with her throat slit and a busted knee cap."

"Wait a second, you don't think *I* . . ."

"She says you're a friend, that's all. She's not accusing you of anything. But I can't help wondering if there might be a connection between what happened to her and the robbery at your place. Call it a cop's instinct."

"You think I'm that connection?"

"I don't think you're responsible, if that makes you feel any better. However, I'd be real interested to see what happens if I get you two together to talk."

Brian shifted nervously on the bed as that ominous feeling—the sense that something bad was lurking just beyond the horizon—returned. "She really wants to talk to me that badly, huh?"

"You're the only one she's willing to talk to."

"All right," Brian said, realizing he didn't have a choice, "let's go." He followed the detective out of the room, rode down the elevator with him, and walked through the underground parking lot to his car.

Donaven flashed his badge at the parking attendant and the attendant waved him through.

The day was warm. Brian rolled down his window to let in some fresh air.

"You know, she's really a lucky girl," the detective finally said.

"How so?"

"Whoever sliced her up took out her vocal chords. Lucky for her, they missed both major arteries. I'm not a doctor, but I'm pretty sure if either of those had been hit, she'd be dead. I still don't get why some dumb fucker would dump her out in the middle of an intersection, though. Maybe he didn't have the balls to finish the job himself and he thought somebody would just run her over. Boom. That would be that."

Brian sighed, but said nothing. As a cop, Donaven had offered up more information than he should have. He was sharing details that Brian didn't want to know.

"One eyewitness said she just appeared out of thin air, literally," the detective continued. ". . . if you can believe that." He chuckled and shook his head.

They pulled into the parking lot and were soon on the third floor of the hospital. Dr. Stort, a short, hairy man with hairy palms, led them into Raven's room.

She was surrounded by machines that seemed to live and breathe with her, for her. Bandages hid stitches on her neck. Her right leg, from thigh to toe, was in a cast.

She turned her attention away from the television when they entered and smiled when she saw Brian. "That's the first smile I've seen from her," Donaven said, as she waved them over.

Cautiously, Brian approached.

Raven reached for the pen and pad on the bedside table.

Hi, she wrote.

"I should warn you, she has trouble with her spelling."

"Hi," Brian said.

Ivv meised yoou, she wrote.

"Do you recognize her now?"

Brian stared hard, reluctant to say he didn't. He could see the desperation in her silvery eyes. She wanted him to remember her. And, to be honest, she looked vaguely familiar. To be completely honest, she looked like the woman in his dream. But dreams, he knew, had no place in a police investigation.

"I don't think so."

Tri, she wrote.

"I'm sorry. I wish I did," he told the detective. "Anything I could do to find John's killer, you know I would. Where should I know her from?"

Donaven shrugged, disappointed.

Raven wrote: *lost angls*

"Where?" he asked her.

Lst engles

Brian looked at Donaven. "I'm sorry I can't be more help." He took a step back.

Raven wrote with desperation: *Waite dont goe Dont goe*

"I can't help you. I wish I could. I do," he said sadly. Then to Donaven: "Both of you. You know I do."

Dont goe

Brian backed toward the door. "I don't know who you are." He turned to leave and she threw the writing supplies at him. The doctor, who'd remained all but invisible until now, ducked. The pen smacked against the wall. The notepad fluttered and tumbled to the floor.

Brian moved faster now, almost racing for the door, and Donaven followed him out.

Back in the room, Raven opened her mouth in a silent, frustrated scream.

CHAPTER 7

Shawn Ryder was quick to notice that Brian was missing on Monday and quick to share the news with the rest of the PR staff at Omega.

"Probably just the flu," Kerri White told Shawn in the break room when he mentioned it to her. She brushed her long red hair away from her face and poured a cup of coffee.

"Yeah, I'm sure that's it," Shawn said. His eyes grew wide. "But what if he was abducted? Like by aliens or something?"

"Oh, don't start in with your stories again. He's probably just sick."

Heating a Pop Tart in the microwave, a portly, shy man from accounting listened but didn't speak.

"Or what if something really bad happened?" Shawn continued. "What if—"

"Stop it, okay? You're being ridiculous. I do wish he'd call, though, and tell us so we'd know how much of his slack we're going to have to pick up." She sipped her coffee and walked out of the room.

But by Tuesday, even Kerri, who had been running the PR department for the last three months, was concerned. She called his home, got no answer, and finally resigned herself to the fact that he might not return. Maybe he had quit . . . or walked out, so to speak.

Suddenly, Timothy Maine, CEO of Omega, charged through the glass door that divided the PR department from the rest of the building. He huffed and puffed with exhaustion. Rage twisted his round, pudgy face and his skin was burning red.

With two security guards in tow, he stopped when he could see that Brian was not at his desk, then barked at Shawn: "Where is Mr. Dore?"

Shawn sank low in his chair. "I don't know. I haven't seen him."

Maine made a sharp right, with the guards still behind, and threw open the door to Kerri's office. He repeated his question.

"He hasn't been in today," she said, struggling to keep her composure. Maine was rude and unpredictable. That unpredictability made him intimidating.

"What about yesterday? He wasn't here yesterday, either, was he?"

“No,” she said.

He sneered and stormed out of the department, cursing.

#

Not thirty minutes ago, Maine had been sitting in his office, tucked comfortably into his big leather chair, enjoying his morning coffee. It had been looking like it was going to be a good morning. *The Wall Street Journal*, which was spread out across his oak desk, had reported his stocks were up. His dog Stew had managed the night without taking a dump on his floor.

You have to take joy in the little things, he said, because the big things take too much time.

His phone rang.

Security had been reviewing the tapes from the weekend. Standard procedure. There was never anything unusual on them. Because of that, the security staff always took their time getting around to the work.

Never . . . until now.

“You need to get down here right away,” Security Officer Bob Jenkins told Maine. “We’ve had a break-in.”

“Where?”

"Sub-level."

Maine nearly choked on his coffee and hung up. *Sub-level?* His heart began to pound. *What the . . . ?*

This wasn't going to be a good morning, after all.

On the way out of his office, he told his secretary to call Steven Lester and have him come down to security. But he didn't slow down to wait for her response or reaction.

Steven Lester was the twitching, stuttering genius behind Omega, the man who'd made even the company's most unlikely projects a success. He was the only scientist Maine had ever known who shared the CEO's unhealthy interest in, well, certain subjects that neither man discussed outside of Maine's office or The Lab.

Sub-level.

Save Maine and Lester, only the guards at Omega knew it existed. The only camera down there watched a plain white hallway and a door that was always closed. No further security had been necessary. Not only were the secrets of that room guarded from all eyes, you needed a key to send the elevator to the sub-level and an access code to get through the door at the end of the hall.

When Maine reached the security room, which was not much bigger than a glorified closet, Steven was already there waiting for him. Crowded by monitors and a stack of digital recorders, the four of them—Maine, Lester, and the two guards—barely fit.

"What have we got?" he asked.

"One man. Male. Coming out."

"In, t-t-too, right?" Steven asked. He looked frazzled. His short brown hair, normally carefully parted, was a mess. Behind his glasses, his eyes seemed to have retreated deeper into his skull.

"No sir, just out."

Timothy Maine and Steven Lester shared a quick and meaningful look. But just as fast, Maine dismissed the guard's statement as an error. Since there was only one way in or out, they must have overlooked the intruder's arrival—or not reviewed enough of the tape.

"Play it," Maine demanded, and a guard clicked a button on the keyboard. The counter on the upper-left monitor began to tick off seconds.

After a moment, the lab door opened. Both Timothy and Steven knew their intruder from just a glance.

Brian Dore. Dressed only in a long white lab coat. Carrying a pill bottle.

"H-H-Holy . . ."

"This is a problem," Maine said.

“A big one,” Steven agreed.

“He remembers the room.”

“Apparently.”

“But how’d he get in?” Maine asked softly, mostly to himself. Then, in a more demanding voice, he told Steven, “Find out what he took.”

To the guards: “Come with me.”

#

Having seen the tape, Maine wasn’t surprised that Brian hadn’t come to work. He sent the guards back to their posts and returned to his office. His first call went out to John Flanders.

By God, *somebody* should have told him about Brian’s absence. As a secret employee of Omega, that old man was responsible for reporting any unusual behavior.

No answer.

His second call went out to a guy who called himself “Rock.” Rock had been a professional boxer for five years and had the mangled, flat nose to prove it. After a ruptured spleen forced his early retirement, he had moved into private investigation.

However, it was neither his size nor brutality Maine

most prized. He was a man without morals. So were the men he hired. For Maine, this was invaluable.

"I've got a job for you," he said into the phone, and slid one hand across the top of his bald head. A ring of gray hair that ran ear to ear was all he had left from his once-impressive blond locks. "I've got an address I need you to check out."

"Sure thing, Mr. Maine. We'll get right on it."

Of course they would. Rock and his associates always gave Maine's problems top priority. Rightly they should, Maine would have said. The CEO paid them three times their normal rate to ensure both their expediency and their discretion.

Tight lips were important when dealing with problems as delicate as his. Problems like his could not be discussed in polite society. He was trying to change the world—for the better, mind you, but . . .

Well, people simply wouldn't understand.

They don't spank kids in school anymore. Even spanking one at home was frowned upon. People were too tolerant these days. Sure, they wanted their fancy homes and their fancy cars, their streets free of crime and their bodies made well when they got sick, but they didn't want to know what dark beasts made those things possible.

After Maine gave Rock the address, he said, "I want the house secured as soon as you arrive. If Mr. Dore's there, hold him until the close of business, then bring him to me. If Flanders is there, find out why he hasn't called."

"I'm on it."

"You bet you are."

#

"I don't know who she is. I don't know why she asked for me," Brian stammered.

He and Donaven were standing in the hall just outside Raven's room when the doctor came out of the door behind them. "I'm sorry, I don't know what's wrong with her," he said. "She hasn't acted like that since she's been here."

"I don't know what she wants from me."

"Calm down," Donaven said. "Take it easy."

Brian ran his hands down his cheeks, tried to nod.

"Why'd you get so freaked out back there?"

"I don't know."

The doctor stepped back to a respectful distance, but not out of earshot. A pack of nurses scurried past, giggling about one thing or another.

"Because she got so mad," Brian added.

Donaven's hands were back on his hips again. "That's all?"

"Well, she did look"—*vaguely like*—"sorta familiar. But I really don't know why."

"All right, take it easy. I'm going to need you to go back in there so I can find out what she has to say—"

"I can't go back in there. You saw how she acted . . ."

"Look, son, you will go back in there. I've got a murder to solve. You need—"

"I can't."

"You'll do it in handcuffs if that's what it takes!" Donaven snapped.

#

Maine hung up the phone and began pacing, his thoughts sifting through his mind too fast to make sense. He stopped at the small bar by his couch, poured a tall bourbon, and downed half of it before Steven came into the room.

Steven looked more alarmed than he had before, though Maine couldn't have said exactly how. Maybe it was because his movements seemed more abrupt. Or maybe it was the slight tremor in his hands. “Jesus,” he said. “F-F-F-Flyin’ Mary, mother of Jesus.”

After another gulp of bourbon, Maine put the glass on his desk. “What?”

“He took a bottle of the Diaxium. There are still two more, but . . .”

Maine sighed with frustration. “Do you think he knows what it does?”

“Do I n-n-need to remind you? We don’t even know what it does.”

Steven was right. All they had were theories, largely based on Princeton physicist Hugh Everett III’s “Many Worlds” idea.

In 1957, Hugh Everett published his “Many Worlds” idea to better explain the relationship between the microscopic and macroscopic worlds. Until that time, it was generally agreed that the former only had meaning by what we observed in the latter, which is the world we interact with daily.

To do this, he created the universal wave function, which allowed him to determine all possible quantum object configurations.

What Lester found especially interesting about his work was that this wave function, which is still used by physicists today, illustrated that everything which can happen, does happen. Quantum physics explains that, before we interact with or observe the particles that make up the world around us, they are actually in *all possible places* at the same time.

Since, within one dimension, we can't actually observe these particles in more than one place, previous theory arbitrarily claimed that all possibilities collapse to only one possibility when we interact with it. It was a way of dealing with an issue that couldn't otherwise be explained. Everett, however, claimed that it is in the space just before every interaction with the world around us when new dimensions are born. In that small window of time, we assume a relationship with those particles, and every other possible relationship with those particles spawns a new dimension where the alternative relationship exists.

And he provided the mathematics to prove it.

Therefore, Lester wondered, if every possibility throughout history that can happen has happened, why should we be privy to only one timeline when it is actually sandwiched between an uncountable number of others? If we could trigger our molecules to behave differently, effectively tune our brains to align with a different set of probabilities, he theorized, we may be able to shift our entire bodies to a neighboring timeline.

Most likely, any variation of the drug would shift us to the same timeline consistently since it would continue to tune us in to that same probability chain.

The implications of successfully developing such a drug were almost unfathomable. It was exactly the kind of global game changer that got Maine and Lester excited. Diaxium could bring them scientific notoriety, of course, but Maine was also confident that it could net billions from government agencies interested in using it for military applications.

"Jumping from this world to that world and back would give a whole new meaning to sneaking up on your enemy," he'd told Steven.

So far, though, they'd only tested the drug on rats. Initial results were promising, but inconclusive.

After ingesting the drug, the rats had vanished. Contorted, sick, they had faded into thin air, suggesting a shift from one dimension to another as Lester had hoped.

Unfortunately, not all of them returned. Of those that did, many returned mangled and half-dead.

So what could Brian want with the pills? How could he even know about them?

Jerry.

Or the room?

He remembers.

But what could he want with them? And, more importantly, how did he get in?

These were the questions that had to be answered.

#

Reluctantly, Brian went back into Raven's room. Her hands had relaxed from knotted fists. She was staring blankly at the wall in front of her. As soon as she heard the door, she turned. Her face lit up. She tried to say something, but Brian couldn't read her lips. With urgent desperation, she mimicked writing something.

Donaven looked from the pad and pen on the floor to Brian and back. "Go on," he prodded.

The doctor slipped in behind them.

More cautious than he'd been before, Brian picked up the writing supplies. He carried them over to Raven. She took them greedily and scribbled out on a fresh page: *Dnt go*

"There was something you wanted to tell him," Donaven reminded her. "Something you would tell only him. What was that?”

She looked from the cop to Brian to the paper to Brian, and turned over a fresh sheet on the pad. Then, again, in big letters: *Dont go*

The more Brian tried to figure out why she looked so familiar, the more he realized she resembled the woman from his dream.

“We’re not going to leave you just yet,” Donaven said.

She turned over another page, and wrote with even bigger letters—

Ddont ggo

Dontt go

Doont goe

CHAPTER 8

"'Don't go.' That's all she kept writing over and over again," Brian told Shawn later that evening. They were sitting in the hotel's restaurant, drinking coffee.

Shawn was one of the few people Brian spent time with other than John. They had bonded over their shared love of tennis and, until recently, had a standing Sunday match. As time passed, he'd come to enjoy Shawn's imaginative stories, even though they often bordered on the absurd. They seemed to color the world in a way that gave every action more meaning than it had on its own. Today, though, Brian needed a sympathetic ear, not conspiracy theories.

"What do you think it meant?" Shawn asked, glancing nervously around. He still had on the blue and white, striped button-down he'd worn to the office, but he had taken off his tie and freed the top two buttons.

"How should I know?"

Shawn glanced to his right again at a nearby diner, sitting by himself, reading a newspaper. "Well, that's not the only strange thing that's happened today. You better be glad you didn't come into the office."

"What happened?"

"Kerri was fired. I was manning her office all afternoon."

"Fired? What for?"

"For not telling Mr. Maine you were absent. Can you believe that? I've seen him go off the deep end before, but today he went nuts. Totally nuts."

"Maybe if I let him know why I've been gone—"

"No way. He had security with him when he came looking for you. That's how he found out you weren't there. He wants your butt bad."

Brian's stomach knotted and he pushed the coffee away. "What for? I haven't done anything to him."

"Jerry got fired too, I heard." Shawn took a sip from his cup. "Bet it had something to do with that conversation he overheard."

"Don't get started on that again."

"I'm just saying—"

"Well, don't."

"Whatever's going on at Omega, Mr. Maine is furious. Heads are rolling, man. I mean really rolling."

"Yeah, I got it."

"So, go ahead. I'm curious. What have you done to make him so mad?"

"Nothing," Brian said defensively. "I don't know why he's mad."

"He showed up with security guards looking for you and you don't know why he's mad?"

"I'd tell you if I did."

"Yeah, well, maybe you would, maybe you wouldn't."

"Let's assume that I would."

They both stopped talking, and a man to their left, alone and reading a book, cleared his throat. Shawn glanced at him, then back at the stranger reading his paper.

"I think you should stay with me tonight. I've got a fold-out couch. It's not fancy, but you'd be comfortable."

"I appreciate that . . . I think I'd just prefer to be alone. Don't get me wrong, I'm glad you came by."

"I think you're making a mistake." Shawn leaned in and whispered, "I'm worried about you. I think we're being watched."

More conspiracy theories.

More fairytales.

"I'm serious." His eyes darted to the right. "The man with the newspaper over there." To the left. "The man with the book over there." Back at Brian. "And one behind you.

He's been working on the same drink since I arrived."

"Shawn."

"I'm just—"

"Listen to me."

"—worried."

"This is a big hotel in a big city. They're probably just here on business. Please . . . please don't start in with more of your stories. Not right now."

"But everything at the office . . . And Mr. Maine is a powerful man."

"I haven't done anything to him. How would he find me at the hotel, anyway?" Brian signed the slip the waiter had left and billed the drinks to his room. He stood up, his chair squealing loudly against the wooden floor as he slid it back. All three men glanced briefly at him. So did a couple at another table.

"Don't stay here tonight," Shawn pleaded, now standing, as well.

"I'll call you tomorrow."

"What if—"

"I will."

The notes, the pills, the girl, the gun . . . No, don't let his stories inside. Not right now. I have enough of my own problems right now. Nobody's watching me.

“You know,” Brian continued, “you should think about chilling out on the stories you tell. You know they’re just fun and games, right?”

Shawn smirked as if it were a joke. “Maybe I do, maybe I don’t.” Then he winked.

They shook hands and Brian walked away. “Thanks for stopping by.”

“You better get in touch with me tomorrow,” Shawn called after him. He glanced one last time at each of the three men—they were a mean-looking bunch.

Shrugging off his suspicion, he headed through the lobby to the front exit.

#

But Brian had let the stories inside.

At the rear of the lobby, he pressed the elevator button and glanced back at the restaurant. The men were still there. A bald man reading his newspaper. A crew cut behind a book. Shaggy blond hair at the bar.

They’re not watching me.

The elevator doors opened and he rode back up to his floor.

He’d spent all afternoon in his room. Trying to sleep.

Twirling the bottle of pills in his hand. Wondering who had left it.

Now, he would try to sleep again. He would try not to think about Flanders, Maine, Shawn, Raven, the note . . .

Everything would make more sense after a good night's sleep.

He stripped to his boxers, turned off the light, and crawled under the covers.

They weren't watching me.

Then his door opened.

CHAPTER 9

The three men had wandered into the restaurant casually, one after the other, several minutes apart. The man with the bald head and flattened nose had been first. Then, his associate with shaggy blond hair. Finally, the crew cut.

Finding Brian had not been without its challenges, but it hadn't been the most difficult job Rock and his partners had done, either.

The journey had begun, of course, at Flanders's house. Though there was no activity there at the time, police tape still marked off the property.

Dressed in a suit, Rock ducked under the tape, put on a pair of black leather gloves, and went in through the unlocked door. Nobody was on the street to observe him. Inside, despite the gloves, he touched nothing.

Enough light filtered in through the windows to make all the rooms visible. Floorboards squeaked under his feet.

He quietly examined each room. The phone was still off the hook in the den. Blood stained the wall and the floor in the hallway.

The kitchen was in shambles. Drawers open. Silverware on the floor. Broken dishes. The overhead lamp was shattered.

Upstairs he found the hole torn into Brian's door; his bedroom window was still open.

When he got back to the car, he called his office.

"Bernhard and Associates," a man answered.

Rock, born Allen Bernhard, looked out his windshield and saw a little girl pull out of a garage on her bike and peddle away. Into the phone, he said, "Frankie."

"You know it, pal. What's up?"

"I need you to get in touch with your guys on the force. Find out what happened at the Flanders address."

"Sure thing. Call you back in ten?"

"Make it five, if you can." Then Rock hung up, turned the key in the ignition until it clicked once, and listened to the radio while he waited for his phone to ring. The little girl on the bike rode back down the street, grinning and laughing. She passed him, turned around, and rode back up again.

"Screw it."

He headed back toward the office. There was no good reason to sit in his car beside a crime scene waiting for a phone call.

#

Just after turning onto Tenth Street, Rock got the call from Frankie Munch that he'd been waiting for. Frankie was an ex-cop, homicide, so getting information usually didn't take long.

He reported the murder to Rock, but said he couldn't find out Brian's whereabouts. Asking for those specifics might raise suspicion from his contacts. Besides, with Rock's second and final associate a computer whiz, a notable hacker at twelve and one of the best in the world at thirty, they didn't need the cops to get Brian's location.

Rock told Frankie to get Crow Gartner, the computer whiz, working on it.

"He's on his way back now," Frankie said.

"From where?"

"He was watching Mrs. Martinez's husband, remember? The suspected affair?"

That's right. The affair. Researching suspected infidelity was beneath them, but it made up much of their work.

"Don't worry," Frankie continued, "I've already called

Hubbard Investigators and got a sub out there for him." Hubbard regularly covered their excess business. "It's just a watch-and-shoot job right now, so any ape they send out there can do it."

"How long will it take him to get back?"

"He should be walking through the door any second."

Rock pulled to a red light. "Fine. Get him working on the brat's location as soon as he walks in the door."

"Will do."

#

Rock's firm was located on the third floor of an old brick building downtown. Other occupants of the building included insurance agencies and a new law firm.

In the twelve hundred square feet Rock had claimed as his, the linoleum tile had started to peel at the corners. The walls needed a new coat of paint. Each of his associates had his own office, but they spent most of their time huddled together in Rock's. No receptionist had sat up front for more than a year; a bell tied to the door announced visitors as effectively as she had.

"I've got it!" Crow shouted. Frankie, still wearing the buzz cut he'd first donned during his years on the force, was in his office seconds later. So was Rock.

Crow had accessed Brian's credit cards with relative ease. "He's at The Embassy Suites. Even got the address for you."

Rock picked up the receiver of Crow's desk phone and called Maine. Now that he had more than just the murder to report, he was prepared for the conversation.

"What have you got for me?" Maine asked.

"Good and bad."

"So? What is it?"

"First, I guess you should know John Flanders is dead."

Maine, who didn't seem even mildly upset by Flanders's death, just asked if they'd located Brian.

"Yes, we have. He's staying at a hotel near John's house."

"Good. The rest of your men are there with you?"

"Yes, sir."

"Put me on speakerphone."

Rock did.

"I want you guys to get down to the hotel, but don't do anything stupid," Maine said. "Find him. Watch him. When it's quiet, bring him to me. And, by God, find the pills he took, too."

And that is exactly what they did.

As Maine had expected, there were too many people in the parking garage, the hallways, and the lobby to do anything but wait. Theirs were not faces they wanted remembered.

One at a time, they followed Brian into the restaurant. If he tried to bolt, they would nab him then, regardless of how it might look. They'd grab Shawn, too, if they had to. Maine would be livid if they let Brian slip away.

But they didn't have to.

After Brian had disappeared into the elevator, after Shawn had left the hotel, the three men casually made their way up to Brian's room. With one quick phone call, Frankie had gotten his room number from the desk clerk on their way over; he'd claimed he was a cop and had the experience to sound legit. Only a minimal amount of intimidation had been necessary. They didn't want the police knocking on every room in the hotel, alarming their guests, did they?

Now, outside of Brian's door, it was Crow's turn to go to work. Years ago, for occasions like these, he had stolen a Hilton keycard, modified it, and wired it to a small black box of his own design. The box had numerous buttons and lights on it. It was essentially a simplified code breaker.

Since most hotel keycards were nearly identical in size, he could make it work just about anywhere.

He removed the device from his briefcase and slid the keycard into the slot on Brian's door. Two six-inch wires ran from the modified card to the black box. He pressed a series of buttons. A red light began to flash. On the digital display, glowing green numbers scrolled through combinations too fast to read. They stopped. The red light blinked off. A bright green light just above it came on. The lock clicked.

#

They weren't watching me, Brian told himself, lying in bed, eyes closed. *They were just hotel guests.*

His door opened fast. Light from the hall shot across the multicolored carpet. He tried to turn over in bed, to get a look at the intruders, but barely saw the three men in suits sweep in before one had a knee in his back. They moved with the speed of demons.

Handcuffs locked around his wrists.

The man with shaggy blond hair opened a briefcase and removed a roll of duct tape. He tore off a piece, which he handed to the man with the crew cut. The crew cut sealed the tape over Brian's mouth while the bald man found the bottle of pills and stuffed it into his coat pocket. Without bothering to dress him, they yanked Brian to his feet and led him out of the room.

He kicked wildly to no avail. His muffled screams dissipated to nothing only feet away.

They escorted him down the hall into the stairwell before they heard a guest open up a door behind them, but they were safely out of sight by then.

On the landing, the crew cut grabbed Brian by the feet while the bald man held him around the chest.

They carried him quickly down four flights, came out into the parking garage. A black van was waiting right outside the door.

They shoved Brian into the back. Two of the men climbed in there with him. The third took the driver's seat.

As late as it was, there was no parking attendant to watch the exit. The wooden arms were raised.

They pulled into traffic, made several sharp turns.

Brian squealed and fought against the knee in his back, even though he knew it was too late to escape. The bald man removed a gun from underneath his blazer. He held it close enough to the floor so that Brian could see it.

Brian stopped squirming. Instead, he looked up

through the tinted windows at the dark sky above. What had happened to his life?

#

Another turn. Another parking garage. Another elevator. As nondescript as all of it was, he had seen this garage, this elevator enough times to recognize them. He was back at Omega.

The bald man inserted a key into a small hole at the base of the keypad and they dropped . . . one floor? Two? Brian couldn't be sure. No matter how many floors it was, though, Brian was surprised to find them going down. Until now, he had believed this elevator could only go up from this floor.

When the doors opened, his kidnappers dragged him down a long white hallway that he had never seen before.

At the end of the hallway was another door. The bald man typed in a code on the adjacent keypad. Like on Crow's homemade code breaker, a red light turned green, permitting access. They took him inside.

Here, the floor was covered with thin gray carpet. Strange machinery crowded the room. A deprivation tank. An electric chair. A slanted steel table with attached leather straps. Something that looked like a cage barely big enough for a person. A long wooden box that reminded Brian of a coffin.

Tall bookshelves full of pill bottles and an untold number of caged rats accented the horrific décor.

Standing dead center in this terrifying space was Mr. Maine. The twitching, stuttering Steven was slightly behind him.

The crew cut and the bald man held him tightly while shaggy closed the door. Then Maine nodded and the bald man ripped the tape off Brian's mouth.

Although he wanted to scream for help, shock kept him silent. Besides, he knew it wouldn't do any good.

The bald man handed Maine the bottle of pills he'd taken from the hotel room. The CEO frowned at them. He passed the bottle to Steven.

"There's a lot of them missing," Steven said.

Maine disregarded the comment. Instead, he looked directly at Brian and asked, "What do you remember?"

Brian breathed through his mouth, trying not to smell the decay, sulfur, and iodine that seemed to hang in the air. Fear held his tongue.

"Do you remember where you're from?"

Finally, he managed a hoarse whisper. "Why shouldn't

I?"

Maine flinched as if he had been struck. Steven crossed his arms and clenched his jaw. "You remember your name?" Maine asked.

"Brian."

Maine leaned forward to better hear the young man. "What?"

"Brian Dore."

He smiled a weird, unnatural smile. "That's right. So, tell me, Brian Dore, how you know about this room. How did you get in here?"

"I've never been here before."

Speaking to Brian as if he were a child, Maine said, "It's not good to lie. We've got you on tape."

"What are you talking about?"

Steven shook the bottle in his hand. "What d-d-did you want with these?"

"I don't even know what they are."

"We could have done so much worse before, Brian. We spared you. This is how you repay us?" Maine asked.

"Please, Mr. Maine," Brian said, confused not only by the entire situation, but by Maine's choice of words, as well. "I really don't know what you're talking about."

The girl, the notes. . . .

“Two days ago everything made sense. Everything was exactly like it was supposed to be.”

The pills, the dream. . . .

“Then someone broke in and killed the man who raised me.”

The blood dripping down the wall. . . .

A tear formed in one eye and rolled down Brian’s cheek. “I don’t understand anything anymore.” He just kept hoping—especially now—that he could go back to sleep and wake up Monday morning to find out this was all a dream. “The pills,” he continued, “somebody left them for me. I don’t know who. I swear, I didn’t know they were Omega’s. I don’t even know what they are.”

“I told you not to lie,” Maine said. “Jerry told everyone about them.”

The Diaxium.

“Like I said, we have you on tape.” He stepped to the side and Steven followed his lead. Brian could now clearly see the long wooden table behind where they had been standing. On it sat a small monitor sandwiched between two humming computers. Maine took control of the mouse. He quickly navigated his way through a series of screens to a virtual control panel. He clicked on the PLAY button. “Sunday night,” he said as the black screen above the control panel came to life.

Brian watched, horrified and confused, as he saw himself move down the white hallway, dressed in just a lab coat, carrying the pills. The only explanation he could imagine, as unlikely as it seemed, was that at some point, during his thirty-hour sleep, he'd executed the theft, met Raven, twisted her into his dream, and convinced himself the pills had been left at an earlier time.

Such a scenario would explain why the pieces of the day hadn't fit together right.

But he was forced to dismiss it. Not only was it as absurd a theory as any Shawn might come up with, it didn't explain the missing gun. And, most importantly, he didn't know about the room!

He didn't have a key for the elevator or the code for the keypad. He simply couldn't have gotten in. The tape must have been manipulated.

Maine stopped the playback and turned off the monitor. "Let's cut through the crap. How many pills have you taken?"

"Just one," Brian said, too scared to lie. The crew cut and the bald man still had a solid grip on him.

"Th-th-there's more than—" Steven pinched his face tight to get the phrase out. "There's more than one missing."

"I swear I only took one."

Maine clasped his hands behind his back and smirked. "Fine, you just took one. What was it like?"

"I had this awful nightmare," Brian said. He sensed that the only way he was going to get out of this situation alive was to tell the truth. "I remember an explosion, crumbling buildings, dirty streets. It all happened so fast. Nobody in the nightmare spoke English, I know that. But I don't know what was going on. It was like they were in the middle of a war."

"Can you be more specific? When the dream started, where were you?"

"I guess it was like . . . like a club."

"What makes you say that?"

"There were flashing lights and music. It just looked like a club."

"Were there people there?"

"Yeah."

"Did any of them notice you when the dream started?"

"Well, they all did," Brian said, nervously.

"Did any of them speak to you?"

"There was this one girl. She spoke to me."

"Could you understand her?"

“No. Like I said, she didn’t speak English.”

“Do you know what language she was speaking?”

Brian thought for a moment, trying to remember her words, the accent. But he couldn’t. His mouth went dry. Despite the cool temperature in the lab, sweat dripped down his face. Maybe it was German, he told himself. However, after meeting the girl in the hospital, he no longer trusted his memory of the dream, no matter how clear it seemed. He must have unconsciously changed her appearance, he told himself. And if that were true, what else might he have changed? “No. I can’t say for sure. I’m sorry.”

“That’s okay,” Maine said, reassuringly. “You’re doing fine.”

However, the fatherly tone only made Brian more uneasy about his situation.

“Then what happened?”

“Then there was an explosion.”

“Really?”

“Really. The whole wall came crashing down and these guys on motorcycles rode in, shooting up the place. Everyone ran. It was chaos.”

“What did you do?”

“The girl. She helped me. She got me out of there.”

"Where did you go?"

"Nowhere." Maine looked skeptical, so Brian explained. "I mean, we got out of the club and into the city. Then we ran. We just ran."

"Interesting. This city you dreamed about. What did it look like?"

"I don't know. I didn't really get a good look at it."

"But you must have seen something."

"I guess it was just like any other big city. I swear—I really don't know how to describe it. I didn't see much."

"And then what happened?"

"I woke up."

"What do you mean? You just woke up?"

"Yeah. I just woke up."

With his hands still clasped behind his back, tapping one finger against his pinky ring, Maine considered Brian's story for some time. While he thought, nobody spoke. Eventually, he asked, "That was the only time you've taken a pill?"

"The only time."

Steven raised a finger, opened his mouth, about to protest.

"How would you feel about taking another one?" Maine asked, before Steven could say anything. "Here. In a controlled environment. Where it's safe."

Nothing about Maine's sub-level lab looked safe to Brian.

"We need to know more about that dream world you wandered into," Maine continued. "It's important . . . for our research."

"But the dream probably won't be the same," Brian said.

"Don't worry yourself about that. As long as you tell us the details of the dream, it doesn't matter what you dream about."

Brian, who had already been trembling, began to feel the vibrations in his legs. He was trapped. His boss was about to experiment on him as if he were one of the rats.

Maine told Steven to get a cup of water and Steven disappeared behind another door.

"Just one time," Maine told Brian in Steven's absence. "Just take one more pill. If you tell us everything when you wake up, every detail, all will be forgiven."

Brian said nothing. Steven returned with a cup of water. He gave it to Maine and took one of the pills from the bottle the bald man had handed over. After he gave that to Maine, too, the CEO moved to within a foot of Brian. "Open your mouth."

Brian trembled, but refused to follow orders.

Maine's eyes shot toward the bald man. "Open his mouth."

Using one hand, the bald man pried Brian's teeth apart. His other hand was locked tightly around Brian's bicep to secure him in place.

Brian wanted to resist, but couldn't. Maine dropped the pill into Brian's mouth and poured the water in after it. Then, without being told, Rock held Brian's mouth shut. He let go of Brian's bicep to clamp his nose, as well.

Seizing the opportunity, Brian thrashed, trying to get free, but the man with the crew cut still had a solid grip on him. With shaggy standing just a few feet behind him, even if he could escape, he wouldn't get far.

As the lack of oxygen took hold, reflex forced down the pill. Immediately after his Adam's apple bobbed, the bald man allowed him to breathe. One long breath. Several more followed—quick and shallow.

Now he was mad. Before he'd been scared, but now he was mad. He'd been violated—poisoned, for all the difference it made. Locking eyes with Maine, he cursed without restraint while uselessly thrashing about, trying to break loose of the men holding him.

If he could escape and vomit up the pill before—

But he couldn't. When he collapsed to his knees, shivering, heart pounding, the two men holding him let go. He began to convulse. Everything went black. He couldn't know that Maine had no plans of releasing him after his trip. He couldn't know, since he thought he was only passing out, that the men in that room watched him fade into nothing.

His boxers and the handcuffs fell to the floor.

#

Because new dimensions—or, as Lester referred to them, probability chains—spin off every fraction of every second, most spin off at points that would not seem significant in and of themselves. That, on one Saturday afternoon in his favorite coffee shop, Maine ordered an espresso in one probability chain and tea in another was not the kind of thing that made or broke kings.

But over time, the rift that divided those two probability chains would expand. Thousands of years later, Lester figured, they would in some ways still reflect each other, while in others be unrecognizably different.

And Maine was anxious for Brian to return and tell them in detail about the one they had tuned him into.

Was it good? Bad? Would he even survive another trip between probability chains?

www.ingramcontent.com/pod-product-compliance
Lightning Source LLC
LaVergne TN
LVHW020650100826
845148LV00012B/2414
9780615861784